THE STREET
That Wasn't There

THE STREET
That Wasn't There

CLIFFORD D. SIMAK
and
CARL JACOBI

ÆGYPAN PRESS

This story was first published in the July, 1941, issue of *Comet*.

Special thanks to Greg Weeks, Sankar Viswanathan, and the
Online Distributed Proofreading Team (which can be found
at http://www.pgdp.net).

The Street That Wasn't There
A publication of
ÆGYPAN PRESS

www.aegypan.com

Mr. Jonathon Chambers left his house on Maple Street at exactly seven o'clock in the evening and set out on the daily walk he had taken, at the same time, come rain or snow, for twenty solid years.

The walk never varied. He paced two blocks down Maple Street, stopped at the Red Star confectionery to buy a Rose Trofero perfecto, then walked to the end of the fourth block on Maple. There he turned right on Lexington, followed Lexington to Oak, down Oak and so by way of Lincoln back to Maple again and to his home.

He didn't walk fast. He took his time. He always returned to his front door at exactly 7:45. No one ever stopped to talk with him. Even the man at the Red Star confectionery, where he bought his cigar, remained silent while the purchase was being made. Mr. Chambers merely tapped on the glass top of the counter with a coin, the man reached in and brought forth the box, and Mr. Chambers took his cigar. That was all.

For people long ago had gathered that Mr. Chambers desired to be left alone. The newer generation of towns-folk called it eccentricity. Certain uncouth persons had a different word for it. The oldsters remembered that this queer looking individual with his black silk muffler, rosewood cane and bowler hat once had been a professor at State University.

A professor of metaphysics, they seemed to recall, or some such outlandish subject. At any rate a furor of some sort was connected with his name . . . at the time an academic scandal. He had written a book, and he had taught the subject matter of that volume to his classes. What that subject matter was, had long been forgotten, but whatever it was had been considered sufficiently revolutionary to cost Mr. Chambers his post at the university.

A silver moon shone over the chimney tops and a chill, impish October wind was rustling the dead leaves when Mr. Chambers started out at seven o'clock.

It was a good night, he told himself, smelling the clean, crisp air of autumn and the faint pungence of distant wood smoke.

He walked unhurriedly, swinging his cane a bit less jauntily than twenty years ago. He tucked the muffler more securely under the rusty old topcoat and pulled his bowler hat more firmly on his head.

He noticed that the street light at the corner of Maple and Jefferson was out and he grumbled a little to himself when he was forced to step off the walk to circle a boarded-off section of newly-laid concrete work before the driveway of 816.

It seemed that he reached the corner of Lexington and Maple just a bit too quickly, but he told himself that this couldn't be. For he never did that. For twenty years, since the year following his expulsion from the university, he had lived by the clock.

The same thing, at the same time, day after day. He had not deliberately set upon such a life of routine. A bachelor, living alone with sufficient money to supply his humble needs, the timed existence had grown on him gradually.

So he turned on Lexington and back on Oak. The dog at the corner of Oak and Jefferson was waiting for him once again and came out snarling and growling, snapping at his heels. But Mr. Chambers pretended not to notice and the beast gave up the chase.

A radio was blaring down the street and faint wisps of what it was blurting floated to Mr. Chambers.

". . . still taking place . . . Empire State building disappeared . . . thin air . . . famed scientist, Dr. Edmund Harcourt. . . ."

The wind whipped the muted words away and Mr. Chambers grumbled to himself. Another one of those fantastic radio dramas, probably. He remembered one from many years before, something about the Martians. And Harcourt! What did Harcourt have to do with it? He was one of the men who had ridiculed the book Mr. Chambers had written.

But he pushed speculation away, sniffed the clean, crisp air again, looked at the familiar things that materialized out of the late autumn darkness as he walked along. For there was nothing . . . absolutely nothing in the world . . . that he would let upset him. That was a tenet he had laid down twenty years ago.

*T*here was a crowd of men in front of the drugstore at the corner of Oak and Lincoln and they were talking excitedly. Mr. Chambers caught some excited words: "It's happening everywhere. . . . What do you think it is. . . . The scientists can't explain. . . ."

But as Mr. Chambers neared them they fell into what seemed an abashed silence and watched him pass. He, on his part, gave them no sign of recognition. That was the way it had been for many years, ever since the people had become convinced that he did not wish to talk.

One of the men half started forward as if to speak to him, but then stepped back and Mr. Chambers continued on his walk.

Back at his own front door he stopped and as he had done a thousand times before drew forth the heavy gold watch from his pocket.

He started violently. It was only 7:30!

For long minutes he stood there staring at the watch in accusation. The timepiece hadn't stopped, for it still ticked audibly.

But 15 minutes too soon! For twenty years, day in, day out, he had started out at seven and returned at a quarter of eight. Now. . . .

It wasn't until then that he realized something else was wrong. He had no cigar. For the first time he had neglected to purchase his evening smoke.

Shaken, muttering to himself, Mr. Chambers let himself in his house and locked the door behind him.

He hung his hat and coat on the rack in the hall and walked slowly into the living room. Dropping into his favorite chair, he shook his head in bewilderment.

Silence filled the room. A silence that was measured by the ticking of the old fashioned pendulum clock on the mantelpiece.

But silence was no strange thing to Mr. Chambers. Once he had loved music . . . the kind of music he could get by tuning in symphonic orchestras on the radio. But the radio stood silent in the corner, the cord out of its socket. Mr. Chambers had pulled it out many years before. To be precise, upon the night when the symphonic broadcast had been interrupted to give a news flash.

He had stopped reading newspapers and magazines too, had exiled himself to a few city blocks. And as the years flowed by, that self exile had become a prison, an intangible, impassable wall bounded by four city blocks by three. Beyond them lay utter, unexplainable terror. Beyond them he never went.

But recluse though he was, he could not on occasion escape from hearing things. Things the newsboy shouted on the streets, things the men talked about on the drugstore corner when they didn't see him coming.

And so he knew that this was the year 1960 and that the wars in Europe and Asia had flamed to an end to be followed by a terrible plague, a plague that even now was sweeping through country after country like wild fire, decimating populations. A plague undoubtedly induced by hunger and privation and the miseries of war.

But those things he put away as items far removed from his own small world. He disregarded them. He pretended he had never heard of them. Others might discuss and worry over them if they wished. To him they simply did not matter.

But there were two things tonight that did matter. Two curious, incredible events. He had arrived home fifteen minutes early. He had forgotten his cigar.

Huddled in the chair, he frowned slowly. It was disquieting to have something like that happen. There must be something wrong. Had his long exile finally turned his mind . . . perhaps just a very little . . . enough to make him queer? Had he lost his sense of proportion, of perspective?

No, he hadn't. Take this room, for example. After twenty years it had come to be as much a part of him as the clothes he wore. Every detail of the room was engraved in his mind with . . . clarity; the old center leg table with its green covering and stained glass lamp;

the mantelpiece with the dusty bric-à-brac; the pendulum clock that told the time of day as well as the day
of the week and month; the elephant ash tray on the
tabaret and, most important of all, the marine print.

Mr. Chambers loved that picture. It had depth, he
always said. It showed an old sailing ship in the fore-
ground on a placid sea. Far in the distance, almost on
the horizon line, was the vague outline of a larger
vessel.

There were other pictures, too. The forest scene above
the fireplace, the old English prints in the corner where
he sat, the Currier and Ives above the radio. But the
ship print was directly in his line of vision. He could
see it without turning his head. He had put it there
because he liked it best.

Further reverie became an effort as Mr. Chambers
felt himself succumbing to weariness. He undressed
and went to bed. For an hour he lay awake, assailed by
vague fears he could neither define nor understand.

When finally he dozed off it was to lose himself in
a series of horrific dreams. He dreamed first that he
was a castaway on a tiny islet in mid-ocean, that the
waters around the island teemed with huge poisonous
sea snakes . . . hydrophinnae . . . and that steadily those
serpents were devouring the island.

In another dream he was pursued by a horror which
he could neither see nor hear, but only could imagine.
And as he sought to flee he stayed in the one place.
His legs worked frantically, pumping like pistons, but
he could make no progress. It was as if he ran upon a
treadway.

Then again the terror descended on him, a black,
unimagined thing and he tried to scream and couldn't.
He opened his mouth and strained his vocal cords and
filled his lungs to bursting with the urge to shriek . . .
but not a sound came from his lips.

*A*ll next day he was uneasy and as he left the house that evening, at precisely seven o'clock, he kept saying to himself: "You must not forget tonight! You must remember to stop and get your cigar!"

The street light at the corner of Jefferson was still out and in front of 816 the cemented driveway was still boarded off. Everything was the same as the night before.

And now, he told himself, the Red Star confectionery is in the next block. I must not forget tonight. To forget twice in a row would be just too much.

He grasped that thought firmly in his mind, strode just a bit more rapidly down the street.

But at the corner he stopped in consternation. Bewildered, he stared down the next block. There was no neon sign, no splash of friendly light upon the sidewalk to mark the little store tucked away in this residential section.

He stared at the street marker and read the word slowly: GRANT. He read it again, unbelieving, for this shouldn't be Grant Street, but Marshall. He had walked two blocks and the confectionery was between Marshall and Grant. He hadn't come to Marshall yet . . . and here was Grant.

Or had he, absent-mindedly, come one block farther than he thought, passed the store as on the night before?

For the first time in twenty years, Mr. Chambers retraced his steps. He walked back to Jefferson, then turned around and went back to Grant again and on to Lexington. Then back to Grant again, where he stood astounded while a single, incredible fact grew slowly in his brain:

There wasn't any confectionery! The block from Marshall to Grant had disappeared!

Now he understood why he had missed the store on the night before, why he had arrived home fifteen minutes early.

On legs that were dead things he stumbled back to his home. He slammed and locked the door behind him and made his way unsteadily to his chair in the corner.

What was this? What did it mean? By what inconceivable necromancy could a paved street with houses, trees and buildings be spirited away and the space it had occupied be closed up?

Was something happening in the world which he, in his secluded life, knew nothing about?

Mr. Chambers shivered, reached to turn up the collar of his coat, then stopped as he realized the room must be warm. A fire blazed merrily in the grate. The cold he felt came from something . . . somewhere else. The cold of fear and horror, the chill of a half whispered thought.

A deathly silence had fallen, a silence still measured by the pendulum clock. And yet a silence that held a different tenor than he had ever sensed before. Not a homey, comfortable silence . . . but a silence that hinted at emptiness and nothingness.

There was something back of this, Mr. Chambers told himself. Something that reached far back into one corner of his brain and demanded recognition. Something tied up with the fragments of talk he had heard on the drugstore corner, bits of news broadcasts he had heard as he walked along the street, the shrieking of the newsboy calling his papers. Something to do with the happenings in the world from which he had excluded himself.

*H*e brought them back to mind now and lingered over the one central theme of the talk he overheard: the wars and plagues. Hints of a Europe and Asia swept almost clean of human life, of the plague ravaging Africa, of its appearance in South America, of the frantic efforts of the United States to prevent its spread into that nation's boundaries.

Millions of people were dead in Europe and Asia, Africa and South America. Billions, perhaps.

And somehow those gruesome statistics seemed tied up with his own experience. Something, somewhere, some part of his earlier life, seemed to hold an explanation. But try as he would his befuddled brain failed to find the answer.

The pendulum clock struck slowly, its every other chime as usual setting up a sympathetic vibration in the pewter vase that stood upon the mantel.

Mr. Chambers got to his feet, strode to the door, opened it and looked out.

Moonlight tessellated the street in black and silver, etching the chimneys and trees against a silvered sky.

But the house directly across the street was not the same. It was strangely lopsided, its dimensions out of proportion, like a house that suddenly had gone mad.

He stared at it in amazement, trying to determine what was wrong with it. He recalled how it had always stood, foursquare, a solid piece of mid-Victorian architecture.

Then, before his eyes, the house righted itself again. Slowly it drew together, ironed out its queer angles, readjusted its dimensions, became once again the stodgy house he knew it had to be.

With a sigh of relief, Mr. Chambers turned back into the hall.

But before he closed the door, he looked again. The house was lopsided . . . as bad, perhaps worse than before!

Gulping in fright, Mr. Chambers slammed the door shut, locked it and double bolted it. Then he went to his bedroom and took two sleeping powders.

His dreams that night were the same as on the night before. Again there was the islet in mid-ocean. Again he was alone upon it. Again the squirming hydrophinnae were eating his foothold piece by piece.

He awoke, body drenched with perspiration. Vague light of early dawn filtered through the window. The clock on the bedside table showed 7:30. For a long time he lay there motionless.

Again the fantastic happenings of the night before came back to haunt him and as he lay there, staring at the windows, he remembered them, one by one. But his mind, still fogged by sleep and astonishment, took the happenings in its stride, mulled over them, lost the keen edge of fantastic terror that lurked around them.

The light through the windows slowly grew brighter. Mr. Chambers slid out of bed, slowly crossed to the window, the cold of the floor biting into his bare feet. He forced himself to look out.

There was nothing outside the window. No shadows. As if there might be a fog. But no fog, however, thick, could hide the apple tree that grew close against the house.

But the tree was there . . . shadowy, indistinct in the grey, with a few withered apples still clinging to its boughs, a few shriveled leaves reluctant to leave the parent branch.

The tree was there now. But it hadn't been when he first had looked. Mr. Chambers was sure of that.

*A*nd now he saw the faint outlines of his neighbor's house . . . but those outlines were all wrong. They didn't jibe and fit together . . . they were out of plumb. As if some giant hand had grasped the house and wrenched it out of true. Like the house he had seen across the street the night before, the house that had painfully righted itself when he thought of how it should look.

Perhaps if he thought of how his neighbor's house should look, it too might right itself. But Mr. Chambers was very weary. Too weary to think about the house.

He turned from the window and dressed slowly. In the living room he slumped into his chair, put his feet on the old cracked ottoman. For a long time he sat, trying to think.

And then, abruptly, something like an electric shock ran through him. Rigid, he sat there, limp inside at the thought. Minutes later he arose and almost ran across the room to the old mahogany bookcase that stood against the wall.

There were many volumes in the case: his beloved classics on the first shelf, his many scientific works on the lower shelves. The second shelf contained but one book. And it was around this book that Mr. Chambers' entire life was centered.

Twenty years ago he had written it and foolishly attempted to teach its philosophy to a class of undergraduates. The newspapers, he remembered, had made a great deal of it at the time. Tongues had been set to wagging. Narrow-minded townsfolk, failing to understand either his philosophy or his aim, but seeing in him another exponent of some anti-rational cult, had forced his expulsion from the school.

It was a simple book, really, dismissed by most authorities as merely the vagaries of an overzealous mind.

Mr. Chambers took it down now, opened its cover and began thumbing slowly through the pages. For a moment the memory of happier days swept over him.

Then his eyes focused on the paragraph, a paragraph written so long ago the very words seemed strange and unreal:

Man himself, by the power of mass suggestion, holds the physical fate of this earth . . . yes, even the universe. Billions of minds seeing trees as trees, houses as houses, streets as streets . . . and not as something else. Minds that see things as they are and have kept things as they were. . . . Destroy those minds and the entire foundation of matter, robbed of its regenerative power, will crumple and slip away like a column of sand. . . .

His eyes followed down the page:

Yet this would have nothing to do with matter itself . . . but only with matter's form. For while the mind of man through long ages may have molded an imagery of that space in which he lives, mind would have little conceivable influence upon the existence of that matter. What exists in our known universe shall exist always and can never be destroyed, only altered or transformed.

But in modern astrophysics and mathematics we gain an insight into the possibility . . . yes probability . . . that there are other dimensions, other brackets of time and space impinging on the one we occupy.

If a pin is thrust into a shadow, would that shadow have any knowledge of the pin? It would not, for in this case the shadow is two dimensional, the pin three dimensional. Yet both occupy the same space.

Granting then that the power of men's minds alone holds this universe, or at least this world in its present form, may we not go farther and envision other minds in some other plane watching us, waiting, waiting craftily for the time they can take over the domination of matter? Such a concept is not impossible. It is a natural conclusion if we accept the double hypothesis: that mind does control the formation of all matter; and that other worlds lie in juxtaposition with ours.

Perhaps we shall come upon a day, far distant, when our plane, our world will dissolve beneath our feet and before our eyes as some stronger intelligence reaches out from the dimensional shadows of the very space we live in and wrests from us the matter which we know to be our own.

*H*e stood astounded beside the bookcase, his eyes staring unseeing into the fire upon the hearth.

He had written that. And because of those words he had been called a heretic, had been compelled to resign his position at the university, had been forced into this hermit life.

A tumultuous idea hammered at him. Men had died by the millions all over the world. Where there had been thousands of minds there now were one or two. A feeble force to hold the form of matter intact.

*T*he plague had swept Europe and Asia almost clean of life, had blighted Africa, had reached South America . . . might even have come to the United States. He remembered the whispers he had heard, the words of the men at the drugstore corner, the buildings disappearing. Something scientists could not explain. But those were merely scraps of information. He did not know the whole story . . . he could not know. He never listened to the radio, never read a newspaper.

But abruptly the whole thing fitted together in his brain like the missing piece of a puzzle into its slot. The significance of it all gripped him with damning clarity.

There were not sufficient minds in existence to retain the material world in its mundane form. Some other power from another dimension was fighting to supersede man's control *and take his universe into its own plane!*

Abruptly Mr. Chambers closed the book, shoved it back in the case and picked up his hat and coat.

He had to know more. He had to find someone who could tell him.

He moved through the hall to the door, emerged into the street. On the walk he looked skyward, trying to make out the sun. But there wasn't any sun . . . only an all pervading greyness that shrouded everything . . . not a grey fog, but a grey emptiness that seemed devoid of life, of any movement.

The walk led to his gate and there it ended, but as he moved forward the sidewalk came into view and the house ahead loomed out of the grey, but a house with differences.

He moved forward rapidly. Visibility extended only a few feet and as he approached them the houses materialized like two dimensional pictures without perspective, like twisted cardboard soldiers lining up for review on a misty morning.

Once he stopped and looked back and saw that the greyness had closed in behind him. The houses were wiped out, the sidewalk faded into nothing.

He shouted, hoping to attract attention. But his voice frightened him. It seemed to ricochet up and into the higher levels of the sky, as if a giant door had been opened to a mighty room high above him.

He went on until he came to the corner of Lexington. There, on the curb, he stopped and stared. The grey wall was thicker there but he did not realize how close it was until he glanced down at his feet and saw there was nothing, nothing at all beyond the curbstone. No dull gleam of wet asphalt, no sign of a street. It was as if all eternity ended here at the corner of Maple and Lexington.

With a wild cry, Mr. Chambers turned and ran. Back down the street he raced, coat streaming after him in the wind, bowler hat bouncing on his head.

Panting, he reached the gate and stumbled up the walk, thankful that it still was there.

On the stoop he stood for a moment, breathing hard. He glanced back over his shoulder and a queer feeling of inner numbness seemed to well over him. At that moment the grey nothingness appeared to thin . . . the enveloping curtain fell away, and he saw. . . .

Vague and indistinct, yet cast in stereoscopic outline, a gigantic city was lined against the darkling sky. It was a city fantastic with cubed domes, spires, and aërial bridges and flying buttresses. Tunnellike streets, flanked on either side by shining metallic ramps and runways, stretched endlessly to the vanishing point. Great shafts of multicolored light probed huge streamers and ellipses above the higher levels.

And beyond, like a final backdrop, rose a titanic wall. It was from that wall . . . from its crenellated parapets and battlements that Mr. Chambers felt the eyes peering at him.

Thousands of eyes glaring down with but a single purpose.

And as he continued to look, something else seemed to take form above that wall. A design this time, that swirled and writhed in the ribbons of radiance and rapidly coalesced into strange geometric features, without definite line or detail. A colossal face, a face of indescribable power and evil, it was, staring down with malevolent composure.

*T*hen the city and the face slid out of focus; the vision faded like a darkened magic-lantern, and the greyness moved in again.

Mr. Chambers pushed open the door of his house. But he did not lock it. There was no need of locks . . . not anymore.

A few coals of fire still smoldered in the grate and going there, he stirred them up, raked away the ash, piled on more wood. The flames leaped merrily, dancing in the chimney's throat.

Without removing his hat and coat, he sank exhausted in his favorite chair, closed his eyes then opened them again.

He sighed with relief as he saw the room was unchanged. Everything in its accustomed place: the clock, the lamp, the elephant ash tray, the marine print on the wall.

Everything was as it should be. The clock measured the silence with its measured ticking; it chimed abruptly and the vase sent up its usual sympathetic vibration.

This was his room, he thought. Rooms acquire the personality of the person who lives in them, become a part of him. This was his world, his own private world, and as such it would be the last to go.

But how long could he . . . his brain . . . maintain its existence?

Mr. Chambers stared at the marine print and for a moment a little breath of reassurance returned to him. *They* couldn't take this away. The rest of the world might dissolve because there was insufficient power of thought to retain its outward form.

But this room was his. He alone had furnished it. He alone, since he had first planned the house's building, had lived here.

This room would stay. It must stay on . . . it must. . . .

He rose from his chair and walked across the room to the bookcase, stood staring at the second shelf with its single volume. His eyes shifted to the top shelf and swift terror gripped him.

For all the books weren't there. A lot of books weren't there! Only the most beloved, the most familiar ones.

So the change already had started here! The unfamiliar books were gone and that fitted in the pattern . . . for it would be the least familiar things that would go first.

Wheeling, he stared across the room. Was it his imagination, or did the lamp on the table blur and begin to fade away?

But as he stared at it, it became clear again, a solid, substantial thing.

For a moment real fear reached out and touched him with chilly fingers. For he knew that this room no longer was proof against the thing that had happened out there on the street.

Or had it really happened? Might not all this exist within his own mind? Might not the street be as it always was, with laughing children and barking dogs? Might not the Red Star confectionery still exist, splashing the street with the red of its neon sign?

Could it be that he was going mad? He had heard whispers when he had passed, whispers the gossiping housewives had not intended him to hear. And he had heard the shouting of boys when he walked by. They thought him mad. Could he be really mad?

But he knew he wasn't mad. He knew that he perhaps was the sanest of all men who walked the earth. For he, and he alone, had foreseen this very thing. And the others had scoffed at him for it.

Somewhere else the children might be playing on a street. But it would be a different street. And the children undoubtedly would be different too.

For the matter of which the street and everything upon it had been formed would now be cast in a different mold, stolen by different minds in a different dimension.

Perhaps we shall come upon a day, far distant, when our plane, our world will dissolve beneath our feet and before our eyes as some stronger intelligence reaches out from the dimensional shadows of the very space we live in and wrests from us the matter which we know to be our own.

But there had been no need to wait for that distant day. Scant years after he had written those prophetic words the thing was happening. Man had played unwittingly into the hands of those other minds in the other dimension. Man had waged a war and war had bred a pestilence. And the whole vast cycle of events was but a detail of a cyclopean plan.

He could see it all now. By an insidious mass hypnosis minions from that other dimension . . . or was it one supreme intelligence . . . had deliberately sown the seeds of dissension. The reduction of the world's mental power had been carefully planned with diabolic premeditation.

On impulse he suddenly turned, crossed the room and opened the connecting door to the bedroom. He stopped on the threshold and a sob forced its way to his lips.

There was no bedroom. Where his stolid four poster and dresser had been there was greyish nothingness.

Like an automaton he turned again and paced to the hall door. Here, too, he found what he had expected. There was no hall, no familiar hat rack and umbrella stand.

Nothing. . . .

Weakly Mr. Chambers moved back to his chair in the corner.

"So here I am," he said, half aloud.

So there he was. Embattled in the last corner of the world that was left to him.

Perhaps there were other men like him, he thought. Men who stood at bay against the emptiness that marked the transition from one dimension to another. Men who had lived close to the things they loved, who had endowed those things with such substantial form by power of mind alone that they now stood out alone against the power of some greater mind.

The street was gone. The rest of his house was gone. This room still retained its form.

This room, he knew, would stay the longest. And when the rest of the room was gone, this corner with his favorite chair would remain. For this was the spot where he had lived for twenty years. The bedroom was for sleeping, the kitchen for eating. This room was for living. This was his last stand.

These were the walls and floors and prints and lamps that had soaked up his will to make them walls and prints and lamps.

He looked out the window into a blank world. His neighbors' houses already were gone. They had not lived with them as he had lived with this room. Their interests had been divided, thinly spread; their thoughts had not been concentrated as his upon an area four blocks by three, or a room fourteen by twelve.

*S*taring through the window, he saw it again. The same vision he had looked upon before and yet different in an indescribable way. There was the city illumined in the sky. There were the elliptical towers and turrets, the cube-shaped domes and battlements. He could see with stereoscopic clarity the aërial bridges, the gleaming avenues sweeping on into infinitude. The vision was nearer this time, but the depth and proportion had changed . . . as if he were viewing it from two concentric angles at the same time.

And the face . . . the face of magnitude . . . of power of cosmic craft and evil. . . .

Mr. Chambers turned his eyes back into the room. The clock was ticking slowly, steadily. The greyness was stealing into the room.

The table and radio were the first to go. They simply faded away and with them went one corner of the room.

And then the elephant ash tray.

"Oh, well," said Mr. Chambers, "I never did like that very well."

Now as he sat there it didn't seem queer to be without the table or the radio. It was as if it were something quite normal. Something one could expect to happen.

Perhaps, if he thought hard enough, he could bring them back.

But, after all, what was the use? One man, alone, could not stand off the irresistible march of nothingness. One man, all alone, simply couldn't do it.

He wondered what the elephant ash tray looked like in that other dimension. It certainly wouldn't be an elephant ash tray nor would the radio be a radio, for perhaps they didn't have ash trays or radios or elephants in the invading dimension.

He wondered, as a matter of fact, what he himself would look like when he finally slipped into the unknown. For he was matter, too, just as the ash tray and radio were matter.

He wondered if he would retain his individuality ... if he still would be a person. Or would he merely be a thing?

There was one answer to all of that. He simply didn't know.

Nothingness advanced upon him, ate its way across the room, stalking him as he sat in the chair underneath the lamp. And he waited for it.

The room, or what was left of it, plunged into dreadful silence.

Mr. Chambers started. The clock had stopped. Funny ... the first time in twenty years.

He leaped from his chair and then sat down again.

The clock hadn't stopped.

It wasn't there.

There was a tingling sensation in his feet.

www.ingramcontent.com/pod-product-compliance
Lightning Source LLC
Chambersburg PA
CBHW031906170626
46807CB00004B/1921